I Was Dreaming
to Come to America

I Was Dreaming to Come to America

Memories from the Ellis Island Oral History Project
Selected and illustrated by Veronica Lawlor
Foreword by Rudolph W. Giuliani, Mayor, New York City

VIKING

This book is dedicated to my teacher,
David J. Passalacqua, with love and appreciation.

ACKNOWLEDGMENTS: I am grateful to all the people who agreed to share their stories with the Ellis Island Oral History Project. I would like to thank David J. Passalacqua, Margaret Hurst, Lisa Pliscou, and Regina Hayes for their advice and encouragement. Thanks also to Paul E. Sigrist, Jr., Dr. Janet Levine, Ph.D., Peter Hom, and Barry Moreno of the National Parks Service for their assistance. —V. L.

VIKING   Published by the Penguin Group
Penguin Books USA Inc., 375 Hudson Street, New York, New York 10014, U.S.A.
Penguin Books Ltd, 27 Wrights Lane, London W8 5TZ, England
Penguin Books Australia Ltd, Ringwood, Victoria, Australia
Penguin Books Canada Ltd, 10 Alcorn Avenue, Toronto, Ontario, Canada M4V 3B2
Penguin Books (N.Z.) Ltd, 182–190 Wairau Road, Auckland 10, New Zealand

Penguin Books Ltd, Registered Offices: Harmondsworth, Middlesex, England

First published by Viking, a division of Penguin Books USA Inc., 1995   10 9 8 7 6 5 4 3 2 1

Copyright © Veronica Lawlor, 1995   Foreword copyright © Rudolph W. Giuliani, 1995   All rights reserved

LIBRARY OF CONGRESS CATALOGING-IN-PUBLICATION DATA
I was dreaming to come to America : memories from the Ellis Island Oral History Project / selected
and illustrated by Veronica Lawlor ; foreword by Rudolph W. Giuliani, mayor, New York City.   p.   cm.
Summary: In their own words, coupled with hand-painted collage illustrations, immigrants recall their arrival
in the United States. Includes brief biographies and facts about the Ellis Island Oral History Project.
ISBN 0-670-86164-2
1. United States—Emigration and immigration—Juvenile literature. 2. Immigrants—United States—Biography—Juvenile
literature. 3. Ellis Island Immigration Station (New York, N.Y.)—History—Juvenile literature. [1. Ellis Island Immigration Station
(New York, N.Y.)—History. 2. United States—Emigration and immigration—History.] I. Lawlor, Veronica. II. Ellis Island
Oral History Project.   JV6450.I5 1995 304.8'092'2—dc20 [B] 95-1281 CIP AC

Grateful acknowledgment is made for permission to reprint excerpts from the following works: *My Life* by Golda Meir.
Copyright © 1975 by Golda Meir. Reprinted by permission of the Putnam Publishing Group and Weidenfeld and Nicolson.
Interview titled "The Reminiscences of Edward Ferro," Columbia University, Oral History Research Office. Used with permission.

Designed by Tom Lynch and Veronica Lawlor   The artwork was done in collage, using hand-painted paper.
Printed in Singapore   Set in New Aster

Foreword

The Statue of Liberty and Ellis Island are universal symbols of promise and opportunity. Generations of immigrants recall the day they first sailed into New York Harbor as the beginning of a new life.

This volume is a rare joy because it gives life to the thoughts and recollections of those new Americans, allowing us to feel the power of these symbols as if for the first time—seeing our shores through their eyes and taking those tentative first steps in their shoes. We share in their rebirth, and America's wondrous potential rings clear in their words and memories.

We are fortunate to live in a country that represents freedom and hope for millions around the world. And we gratefully bear the burden of ensuring that Liberty's torch will continue to burn for generations of Americans yet to come.

Rudolph W. Giuliani
MAYOR
NEW YORK CITY

About Ellis Island and the Oral History Project

On January 1, 1892, Annie Moore, a 15-year-old girl from County Cork, Ireland, was the first immigrant to land at Ellis Island, America's newest immigration processing center. Situated on a small island in the upper New York Bay, Ellis Island was to become the main port of entry for over 12 million immigrants who passed through its doors until its closing in 1954.

Upon landing at Ellis Island, an immigrant was examined by a doctor to check for serious health problems or contagious disease. If he or she was in good health, the immigrant would then report to a government inspector, whose job it was to determine if that person was eligible for admittance to America, based on U.S. immigration laws. Immigrants denied access to America had the right to appeal their case to the Treasury Department in Washington, D.C. If passed by the doctors and the inspector, immigrants were usually processed in about five hours and admitted to the United States. Others were detained for treatment in one of the island hospitals, held until relatives came to claim them, scheduled for legal hearings, or, in 2 percent of the cases, refused admittance.

After its closing in 1954, Ellis Island was left to the elements and to vandals. In 1965, President Lyndon B. Johnson declared it a national monument, and in 1983, the National Parks Service began its restoration. Opened as a museum in 1990, Ellis Island is truly a tribute to the "melting pot" that is America.

The Ellis Island Oral History Project began in 1973 as an informal collection of interviews with people who had immigrated to this country through Ellis Island. The project picked up steam in the late 1980s with the restoration and preservation of Ellis Island by the National Parks Service. Over 1,200 interviews are on file; more than half of them have been conducted since 1990.

The interviews span a wide range of experiences and include the memories of people from all over the world. Many describe their first impressions of Ellis Island and of America from the perspective of the child they were then; others interviewed came to this country as adults. The interviews explore living conditions in the old country, the voyage to America, and experiences on Ellis Island, as well as early years in the United States, overcoming language barriers, and struggling to make ends meet.

Some of those interviewed were detained at Ellis Island for medical reasons; others were detained for political reasons, primarily during the 1940s and 1950s. Interviews with employees who worked on the island are also included.

The Oral History Library is a national treasure of our cultural heritage. It is an invaluable resource for students of American history, as well as for those who want a better understanding of the immigrant experience. For more information on the Ellis Island Oral History Project, write to:

Ellis Island Oral History Project
Ellis Island Immigration Museum
New York, New York 10004

"My first impressions of the new world will always remain etched in my memory, particularly that hazy October morning when I first saw Ellis Island. The steamer Florida, *14 days out of Naples, filled to capacity with 1,600 natives of Italy, had weathered one of the worst storms in our captain's memory. Glad we were, both children and grown-ups, to leave the open sea and come at last through the narrows into the bay.*

"My mother, my stepfather, my brother Giuseppe, and my two sisters, Liberta and Helvetia, all of us together, happy that we had come through the storm safely, clustered on the foredeck for fear of separation and looked with wonder on this miraculous land of our dreams."

EDWARD CORSI
ITALY
ARRIVED IN 1907 • AGE 10

"My father, who had by now moved from New York to Milwaukee, was barely making a living. He wrote back that he hoped to get a job working on the railway and soon he would have enough money for our tickets....I can remember only the hustle and bustle of those last weeks in Pinsk, the farewells from the family, the embraces and the tears. Going to America then was almost like going to the moon.... We were all bound for places about which we knew nothing at all and for a country that was totally strange to us."

GOLDA MEIR
RUSSIA
ARRIVED IN 1906 • AGE 8

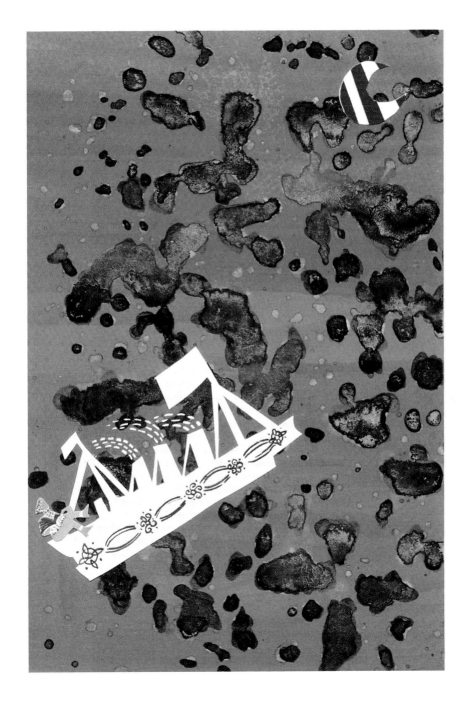

"It was quite a large embarkation, but it was crowded with immigrants. Especially the third class—the so-called steerage class—it was very crowded. But we managed.

"[The] time between meals was spent on the deck if the weather was good. In the evening there was usually dancing and music. Some immigrant would always come out with a harmonica or some musical instrument and the dance would follow. And during the day, of course, there were always acquaintances to be made, discussions about America, the conditions in America, and preparation for life in America. Right among the people themselves, I circulated around quite a bit. I knew a few words in English, in French, and in German already at that time, so I was able to understand some of the talk, even from the sailors."

PAUL STURMAN
CZECHOSLOVAKIA
ARRIVED IN 1920 • AGE 16

"When I was about 10 years old I said, 'I have to go to America.' Because my uncles were here already, and it kind of got me that I want to go to America, too.... I was dreaming about it. I was writing to my uncles, I said I wish one day I'll be in America. I was dreaming to come to America.... And I was dreaming, and my dream came true. When I came here, I was in a different world. It was so peaceful. It was quiet. You were not afraid to go out in the middle of the night.... I'm free. I'm just like a bird. You can fly and land on any tree and you're free."

HELEN COHEN
POLAND
ARRIVED IN 1920 · AGE 20

"I never saw such a big building [Ellis Island]—the size of it. I think the size of it got me. According to the houses I left in my town, this was like a whole city in one, in one building. It was an enormous thing to see, I tell you. I almost felt smaller than I am to see that beautiful [building], it looked beautiful.

"My basket, my little basket, that's all I had with me. There was hardly any things. My mother gave me the sorrah *[a kind of sandwich], and I had one change of clothes. That's what I brought from Europe."*

CELIA ADLER
RUSSIA
ARRIVED IN 1914 • AGE 12

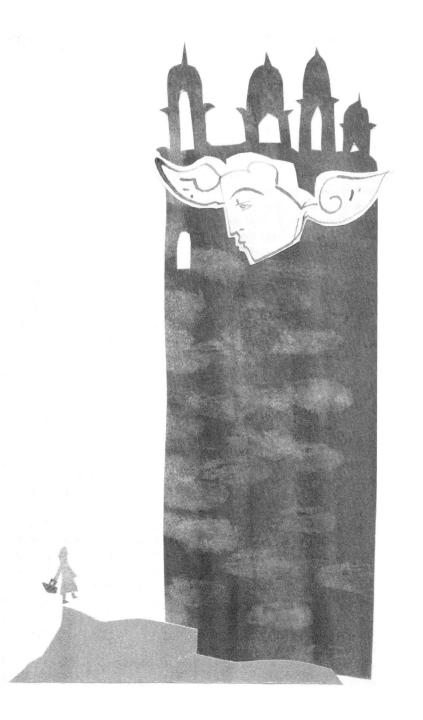

"Most dear to me are the shoes my mother wore when she first set foot on the soil of America....She landed in America in those shoes and somehow or the other she felt that she was going to hang on to them. They are brown high-top shoes that had been soled and resoled and stitched and mended in Sweden to hold them together till she could get to America. We just kept them. And then...as I grew up and everything, I said, 'Don't ever throw them away.'"

BIRGITTA HEDMAN FICHTER
SWEDEN
ARRIVED IN 1924 • AGE 6

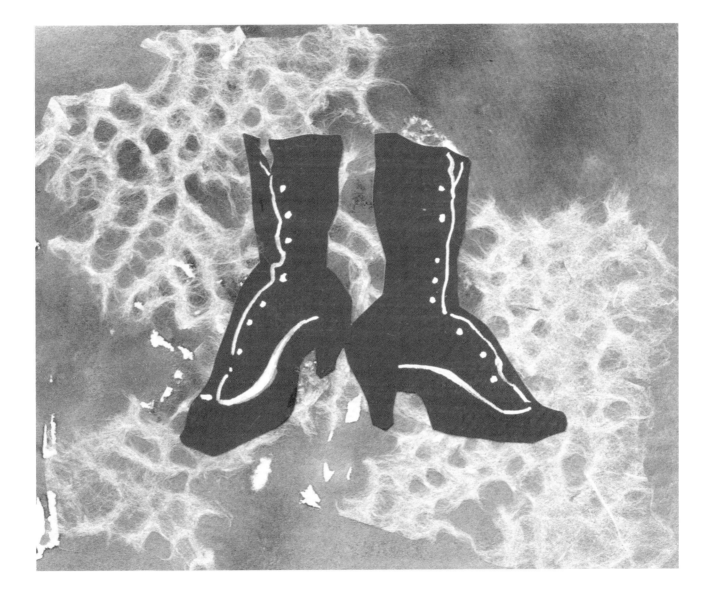

"Coming to America had meaning. I was a kid of seven and in contrast to what I had gone through, Ellis Island was like not a haven, but a heaven. I don't remember any fright when I got to Ellis Island.

"My father's dream and prayer always was 'I must get my family to America.'... America was paradise, the streets were covered with gold. And when we arrived here, and when we landed from Ellis Island and [went] to Buffalo, it was as if God's great promise had been fulfilled that we would eventually find freedom."

VARTAN HARTUNIAN
TURKEY (ARMENIAN)
ARRIVED IN 1922 • AGE 7

"There's just so much confusion.... We had interpreters and most of them were the Traveler's Aid. Let me tell you, they're wonderful. They helped us out every way they could and reassured us, which we needed very badly. Especially, like when we were getting off of Ellis Island, we had all sorts of tags on us—now that I think of it, we must have looked like marked-down merchandise in Gimbel's basement store or something. 'Where are you going, who's waiting for you?' and all that and then we were put in groups and our group was going to the Erie Railroad station in Jersey City."

ANN VIDA
HUNGARY
ARRIVED IN 1921 • AGE 10

"The language was a problem of course, but it was overcome by the use of interpreters. We had interpreters on the island who spoke practically every language.

"It would happen sometimes that these interpreters—some of them—were really softhearted people and hated to see people being deported, and they would, at times, help the aliens by interpreting in such a manner as to benefit the alien and not the government.

"Unless you saw it, you couldn't visualize the misery of these people who came to the United States from Europe....They were tired; they had gone through an awful lot of hardships. It's impossible for anyone who had not gone through the experience to imagine what it was."

EDWARD FERRO
INSPECTOR, ELLIS ISLAND
ITALY
ARRIVED IN 1906 • AGE 12

"It seems to me now, as I look back, that in those days there were crying and laughing and singing all the time at Ellis Island. Very often brides came over to marry here, and of course we had to act as witnesses. I have no count, but I'm sure I must have helped at hundreds and hundreds of weddings of all nationalities and all types.

"There is a post at Ellis Island which through long usage has come to earn the name of 'the Kissing Post.' It is probably the spot of greatest interest on the island, and if the immigrants recall it afterward it is always, I am sure, with fondness. For myself, I found it a real joy to watch some of the tender scenes that took place there…where friends, sweethearts, husbands and wives, parents and children would embrace and kiss and shed tears for pure joy."

FRANK MARTOCCI
INSPECTOR, ELLIS ISLAND
ITALY
ARRIVED IN 1897 • AGE 30

"There was a man that came around every morning and every afternoon, about ten o'clock in the morning and three o'clock in the afternoon, with a stainless-steel cart, sort of like a Good Humor cart…and he had warm milk for the kids. And they would blow a whistle or ring a bell and all the kids would line up. He had small little paper cups and he had a dipper and every kid got a little milk, warm milk. That was one thing that sticks in my mind."

DONALD ROBERTS
WALES
ARRIVED IN 1925 • AGE 12

"And then we settled at Ellis Island there, we stayed there… My sister took sick, I took sick, my other sister took sick…I had a low-grade temperature and my eyes were red. I wasn't used to the electric lights, I suppose. Different environment, you know.

"We got oatmeal for breakfast, and I didn't know what it was, with the brown sugar on it, you know. So I couldn't get myself to eat it. So I put it on the windowsill [and] let the birds eat it."

ORESTE TEGLIA
ITALY
ARRIVED IN 1916 • AGE 12

"I feel like I had two lives. You plant something in the ground, it has its roots, and then you transplant it where it stays permanently. That's what happened to me. You put an end…and forget about your childhood; I became a man here. All of a sudden, I started life new, amongst people whose language I didn't understand.…[It was a] different life; everything was different…but I never despaired, I was optimistic.

"And this is the only country where you're not a stranger, because we are all strangers. It's only a matter of time who got here first."

LAZARUS SALAMON
HUNGARY
ARRIVED IN 1920 • AGE 16

"My father left when I was two years old for America. I didn't know what he looked like. I didn't have the least idea....Then I saw this man coming forward and he was beautiful. I didn't know he was my father. He was tall, slender, and he had brown, wavy hair and to me he looked beautiful. He looked very familiar to me. Later on I realized why he looked familiar to me. He looked exactly like I did."

KATHARINE BEYCHOK
RUSSIA
ARRIVED IN 1910 • AGE 10

"When I got here at Ellis Island, for three days on that island I slept there, I ate there for three days....But for that time, [it] was awfully bad. Scary. Because you don't have no mother no more, you've taken off from the mother and father. You're traveling on your own.

"I mean, you leave your mother, you cry...you cry for your mother all the time, so I wrote a letter to my mother from in the Ellis Island. Told my mother that I got off, I got a job. And it made my mother strong."

FELICE TALDONE
ITALY
ARRIVED IN 1924 • AGE 19

Biographies

....

EDWARD CORSI (page 8) was born in the town of Capestrano, Italy, in 1896. His father died in 1903, shortly after being elected the Tuscan representative to the Italian parliament. Four years later, Corsi's mother remarried, and along with his two sisters and his brother, his mother, and his stepfather, 10-year-old Edward Corsi came to America.

His association with Ellis Island did not end there, however. In 1931, Mr. Corsi was appointed commissioner of immigration at Ellis Island, a position he held until 1934, when he became the director of relief in New York City under Mayor Fiorello H. LaGuardia. Mr. Corsi wrote a book about his experiences, titled *In the Shadow of Liberty: The Chronicle of Ellis Island* (The Macmillan Co., 1935).

GOLDA MEIR (page 10) was born in Kiev, Russia, in 1898. At the age of eight she came to America, along with her mother and her two sisters, to meet her father in Milwaukee. In 1921, Ms. Meir emigrated to Palestine, and was instrumental in establishing the state of Israel in 1948.

She was elected to the Knesset in 1949 and became Israel's foreign minister in 1956. Ten years later, she was elected general secretary of the Mapai party, and became prime minister in 1969, a position she held until her retirement in 1974.

PAUL STURMAN (page 12) came to America from Czechoslovakia in 1920, when he was 16 years old. His father, a cheese maker, had come to the United States in 1913 after his business had failed. Paul, his mother, brother, and two sisters were not able to join him until after World War I. They were detained on Ellis Island for two and a half days, until Paul's father came and claimed them. Paul was married in 1926.

HELEN COHEN (page 14) was born in 1900 to a tailor and his wife in the town of Susnowiec, Poland. The family owned a general store but lost it during World War I. Helen's uncles were already in the United States, and when Helen was 20 she and her father and her youngest brother came to America to join them. They spent 10 days on Ellis Island and heard the celebrated opera singer Enrico Caruso perform there on Christmas Eve.

The family settled in Washington, D.C., where Ms. Cohen worked as a salesperson in a hat store. In 1923 she married a man from Russia, and they had twin girls in 1925. At the age of 25, Ms. Cohen became a U.S. citizen.

CELIA ADLER (page 16) came to the United States from Russia in 1914, when she was 12 years old. She made the trip alone, with only a small basket of food and clothing that her mother had packed for her. After staying with her sister in Bayonne, New Jersey, for a while, Ms. Adler settled in New York City, where she worked as a dressmaker. She eventually married and in the mid-1940s became a U.S. citizen.

BIRGITTA HEDMAN FICHTER (page 18) was born in Sweden in 1917. In 1924, at age six, she came to America with her family aboard the *Jutteningholm*. They spent one night on Ellis Island and, after a brief stay in Vermont, settled in New Jersey. Birgitta married Leslie Fichter in 1938, and they had one son, Gary. She eventually became a real-estate agent in New Jersey.

Mrs. Fichter has appeared on CBS television to share her immigration experience. Her mother's shoes, as well as other family heirlooms, are on permanent display at the Ellis Island immigration museum.

VARTAN HARTUNIAN (page 20) was born in 1915 in Marash, Turkey, to a minister of the Armenian Evangelical Church and his wife. At the time, Armenians were subject to harsh political and religious persecution, and in 1922 Vartan and his family escaped to America via Smyrna and Greece. Upon arriving in America, the Hartunian family was detained on Ellis Island for 12 days while a medical condition affecting the parents' eyes was cleared up. In addition, the quota of Syrians admitted to the U.S. for that year had already been filled. After a 12-day waiting period, Vartan's mother, a Syrian, was admitted because of her profession, teaching.

The family spent a few months in Buffalo before settling in Philadelphia. Vartan graduated from Swarthmore College with honors and became a minister like his father, Abraham. In 1968, Beacon Press published Abraham's memoirs, *Neither to Laugh Nor to Weep*, which Vartan had translated into English.

ANN VIDA (page 22) was born in 1911 in a little village in northern Hungary. In 1921, when Ann was 10 years old, she and her mother traveled aboard the *Beringaria* to America to join her father, who was already employed as a steelworker in Warren, Ohio. Ann married in 1930 and became a U.S. citizen in 1949.

EDWARD FERRO (page 24) was born in the town of Marineo in Palermo, Sicily, in 1894. In 1906, 12-year-old Edward immigrated to America with his mother and his five brothers and sisters to join his father, a physician who had come to New York six months earlier.

Edward Ferro graduated from Columbia University in 1914, and became a pharmacist. After serving in the air force during World War I, Mr. Ferro decided that he no longer wanted to work in a pharmacy. He passed the Immigration and Naturalization Services examination for interpreter, and was appointed an interpreter on Ellis Island in 1920. Six months later he became an inspector.

FRANK MARTOCCI (page 26) was born in Italy in 1867, and immigrated to America in 1897. He worked as an interpreter and then as an immigrant inspector on Ellis Island from the 1890s to the early 1930s. He spoke Italian, French, Spanish, German, and Polish. In 1907, Mr. Martocci trained Fiorello LaGuardia, future mayor of New York, as an interpreter.

DONALD ROBERTS (page 28) was born in 1913 in a mining village in Wales. Food was scarce, and in the spring of 1925 his family sailed to America on board the *Aquatania*. Donald was 12 years old. They were detained on Ellis Island for two weeks while Donald's mother was hospitalized with bronchitis, and then settled in Rutherford, New Jersey.

ORESTE TEGLIA (page 30) was born in 1903, in northern Italy. Oreste's father, who had come to America earlier, worked for the railroads, laying tracks for a dollar a day. In 1916, when Oreste was 12, the family joined Mr. Teglia in America,

leaving their dog, Pisarino, behind. They were held on Ellis Island for three weeks while Oreste and his two sisters were treated for colds.

The family settled in Chicago, and in 1928 Oreste was married. He held many jobs, including working in a nut factory, his cousin's candy store, and in the alterations department at Rothschild's. He became a citizen in 1936.

LAZARUS SALAMON (page 32) was born in the Transylvania section of Hungary in 1904. He had a hard childhood; Romanian soldiers came and took his father away, and his mother died soon after. In 1920, Lazarus, his brother, and one of his sisters traveled to America aboard the *Zeeland*. Lazarus was 16 at the time. They settled in the Yorkville section of Manhattan, and Lazarus eventually became a salesman. He married in 1929.

The father of **KATHARINE BEYCHOK** (page 34) left Russia in 1902 to escape the Russo-Japanese war. At the time, Katherine was only two. She met him again in 1910, when she and her mother and sister came to America to be with him. By then she was ten years old.

Katharine and her family spent three days on Ellis Island because the doctors suspected that her sister had trachoma, an eye disease that could bar a person from entering America. After Katharine's sister was cleared, the reunited family settled in Rochester, New York.

FELICE TALDONE (page 36) was born in Giovinazzo, Italy, in 1906. His father went to America, where he died in 1909. When Felice was 19, he traveled to America hoping to earn a better living and to find where his father had lived and died. He left behind his mother and stepfather and their children.

He arrived at Ellis Island in 1924 and was detained for a few days. At first Felice delivered ice for his uncle, but eventually he became a contractor. He married in 1937, and he and his wife had nine children.

....

Most of the information in these biographies was obtained from interviews conducted by oral historians at Ellis Island. The biographies reflect the varying length and depth of the interviews themselves.